Swim, Boots, Swim!

by Phoebe Beinstein   illustrated by Robert Roper

Simon Spotlight/Nickelodeon
New York   London   Toronto   Sydney

Based on the TV series *Dora the Explorer*® as seen on Nick Jr.®

SIMON SPOTLIGHT
An imprint of Simon & Schuster Children's Publishing Division
1230 Avenue of the Americas, New York, New York 10020
© 2009 Viacom International Inc. All rights reserved.
NICK JR., *Dora the Explorer*, and all related titles, logos, and characters are registered
trademarks of Viacom International Inc. All rights reserved, including the right of
reproduction in whole or in part in any form.
SIMON SPOTLIGHT and colophon are registered trademarks of Simon & Schuster, Inc.
Manufactured in the United States of America
10
ISBN: 978-1-4169-7195-5
0411 LAK

¡Hola! I'm Dora. I'm going to the beach today. My *mami* bought me this bathing suit for the trip. I can't wait to go swimming in the ocean with Boots! Will you come too? Great! *¡Vámonos!* Let's go!

Boots says he can't come to the ocean with me because he doesn't know how to swim.

Don't worry, Boots! My friend Mariana the Mermaid can teach you. She's great at swimming! And swimming is easy once you know how to do it.

Let's head to the beach. Who do we ask for help when we don't know where to go? *¡Sí!* Map!

Map says we have to go over Flying Fish Bridge and through the Silver Sand Dunes to get to the ocean.

We found the Flying Fish Bridge. Whoa, look at all those flying fish! What colors of flying fish do you see? Say them with me. Orange! Blue! Green! Purple! *¡Anaranjado! ¡Azul! ¡Verde! ¡Morado!*

To get across the bridge, we have to duck under the flying fish. Let's count the fish as we go under them. *Uno, dos, tres, cuatro, cinco. ¡Muy bien!* We made it past the bridge. Now we have to find the Silver Sand Dunes.

It's so bright out that I can't see the Silver Sand Dunes. Maybe there's something in Backpack to help us see when the sun is too bright. Let's check. Say "Backpack!"

Do you see something that will help us see in the bright sun? *¡Sí!* Sunglasses! Good thinking!

We look great in our sunglasses! And we found our way to the Silver Sand Dunes Maze. Look at all of the sand dunes!

Help us find our way through the Silver Sand Dunes! Where is the way out? *¡Gracias!*

We made it to the ocean! And there's Mariana the Mermaid waiting for us.

It's time to jump in the water.
Let's swim! *¡Vamos a nadar!*

First, Mariana's going to teach Boots how to go underwater.

She says he has to take a deep breath, hold it, and then lower his head under the water. Great job, Boots!

Now Mariana holds Boots while he moves his arms in the water. Will you move your arms with him? Great job!

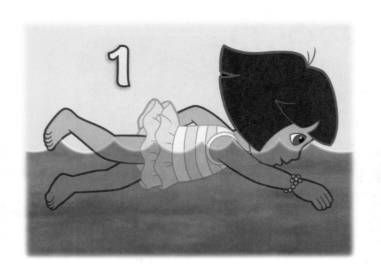

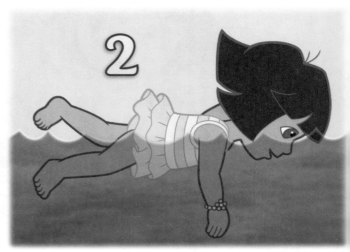

Now she's showing him how to kick his legs. Good strong kicks, Boots!

Wow, Boots can swim all by himself now!

Mariana is a great swimming teacher, and Boots is a fast learner.

What a fantastic day. I love swimming, and now Boots does too. We couldn't have done it without Mariana . . . and *you*. Thanks for helping. *¡Gracias!*